TO SUSAN

LOOK, THERE IS
A TURTLE FLYING

Look, There is a Turtle Flying

STORY AND PICTURES BY

JANINA DOMANSKA

THE MACMILLAN COMPANY, NEW YORK

COLLIER-MACMILLAN LIMITED, LONDON

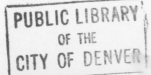

LOOK, THERE IS A TURTLE FLYING

Many years ago, in Poland, King Powoj lived in his castle on Lake Goplo. The King liked to talk to his people as he sat by the lake where the fish swam in the clear water and tall-crested herons sunned themselves.

Sometimes, when the people had

gone, the King would play his lute.

But more than anything else, King Powoj enjoyed talking

to Solon, his pet turtle, who was over a hundred years old.

One warm afternoon, as the sun was laying a

golden carpet across the water, the King said to

Solon, "What are you thinking, Wise One?"

Solon, who was thinking how nice it must be to

fly, snapped, "I was thinking you talk too much."

King Powoj was so surprised that his crown fell off.

He caught it just before it fell into the water.

"You talk all day," said Solon. "I only talk when

I'm spoken to. That is why I will live for hundreds

of years. I save my breath by not talking."

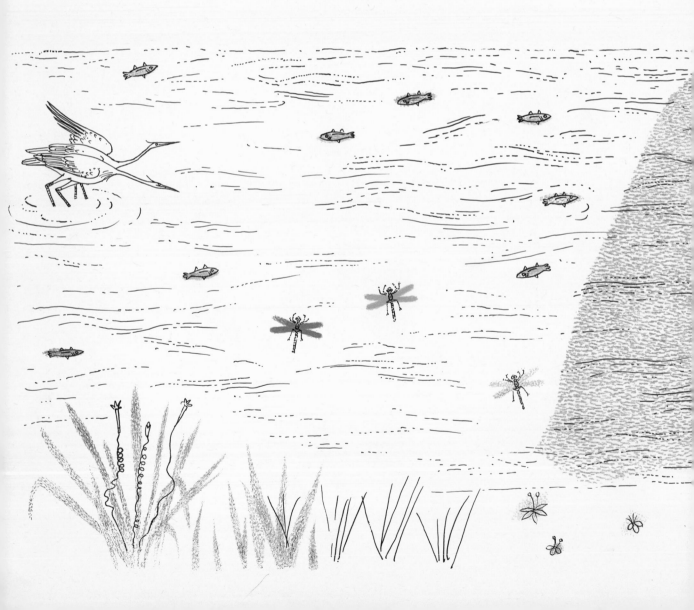

The King was very hurt but he said nothing. Later when

Heba and Helen, his favorite herons, glided down for

a visit, he said with a smile, "I shouldn't talk to you.

Solon says I talk too much." The herons were indignant.

"How dare he say that?" they cried. "He talks more

than Your Majesty."

As they flew away, Heba said, "I'd like

to teach that old turtle a lesson."

The next day, when the two birds were resting in

the reeds, Solon called to them. "I was watching you

fly," he said with a turtle grin. "You're the most

graceful birds. I want to fly too. You're going to

help me. Meet me here tomorrow."

"Of course, Mr. Solon," said Heba. She winked

at Helen. "We will be pleased to help you."

The following afternoon Solon came back carrying a long

stick. "Now listen to me, my winged friends," he said.

"You each take one end of this stick in your beaks and I

will hang on to the middle with my strong teeth."

"You're not afraid of falling?" asked Helen.

"It will be hard to fly without wings. And you

won't be able to talk."

Solon gave them his best wise turtle smile. "Don't

worry about me. I am not like the King, who

talks all the time. I know when not to talk."

He told the two birds to circle the city first and
then fly low over the lake in front of the King.
The turtle was heavy but the herons managed
to lift him.

As they circled above the city the people cried,
"Look, there's a turtle flying! Did you ever
see anything like that?"

Solon was delighted to be the first flying turtle in the whole world.

He was annoyed when the herons flew back toward the lake.

"They should have flown lower so people could recognize me," he

thought. "I shall make the silly things go back."

But he dared not open his mouth. In vain he tried

to attract the birds' attention. When they were back

over the lake, Solon lost his temper. "Hey, foolish

birds," he cried. "Fly lower so the King can see me!"

Heba and Helen never heard him. They just saw

the big splash the vain, old turtle made as he

hit the water. The King had seen it too.

Late that evening Solon climbed wearily ashore.

The King put down his lute.

"Now what are you thinking, Wise One?" he asked.

"I was thinking I talk too much, not you. The next time I fly, I shall keep my mouth shut," replied Solon.

"Ah," said King Powoj, picking up his lute.

"On second thought, I don't think I shall fly again,"

said Solon. "You might have something you wanted to

say to me, and I should be around to hear it."

And Solon smiled a turtle smile.